Ukulele
Hayley

Ukulele Hayley

by Judy Cox

illustrated by
Amanda Haley

Holiday House / New York

Library of Congress Cataloging-in-Publication Data
Cox, Judy.
Ukulele Hayley / by Judy Cox ; illustrated by Amanda Haley. — First edition.
    pages cm
Summary: To save the ukulele band, third-grader Hayley and her classmates protest the
school board's decision to cut funding for the music program. Includes tips on how to play the
ukulele.
ISBN 978-0-8234-2863-2 (hardcover)
[1. Ukulele—Fiction. 2. Music—Fiction. 3. Schools—Fiction.] I. Haley, Amanda, illustrator. II.
Title.
PZ7.C83835Uk 2013
[Fic]—dc23
2012045825

To Tim, who has played an instrumental role in my life.

Also by Judy Cox

Butterfly Buddies

Carmen Learns English

Cinco de Mouse-O!

Go to Sleep, Groundhog!

Haunted House, Haunted Mouse

My Family Plays Music

Nora and the Texas Terror

One Is a Feast for Mouse

Puppy Power

The Secret Chicken Society

Snow Day for Mouse

*That Crazy Eddie and
the Science Project of Doom*

CONTENTS

Ukulele
Hayley

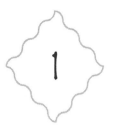

Hidden Talent?

On the first day of school, Hayley trailed the line of third graders down the hallway. Around the corner. Through the double doors. On their way to music.

"Shrimp!" whispered Skeeter.

Hayley made a face. She hated that nickname. Why did Mrs. McCann have to line them up by size? *It isn't fair,* thought Hayley. All summer she had done everything she could to grow. She had eaten second helpings. She had played soccer. She had done exercises. Last night Mom had measured her, and she'd grown an inch and a half!

But when the third graders lined up, Hayley saw the other kids had grown too. They towered over her. Even Skeeter had grown.

Skeeter had been Hayley's friend since kindergarten. His real name was Scott, but everyone called him Skeeter. Hayley thought it was perfect. For as long as she could remember, Skeeter had been hanging around. Bugging her, just like a mosquito.

"You're the runt, now," Skeeter pointed out.

I'm only one inch shorter than you, she thought. But she couldn't seem to get the words out. Too shy. Again.

At first Hayley and Skeeter had been the same height—the shortest kids in kindergarten, first, and even second grades. But this summer, when she went to the amusement park with Skeeter and his family, Hayley noticed a change.

Everyone wanted to ride the Monster Masher, but the sign read, "You must be this tall to ride." Hayley missed it by half an inch. Skeeter made it by half an inch.

He laughed as he boarded the ride. "Shrimp!" he teased. Served him right that he had thrown up afterward!

Hayley was still thinking about that as the line of third graders snaked down the hall past Ms. Lyons, the school principal. Hayley knew Ms. Lyons, but the man standing next to her was a stranger.

Unlike most teachers, he wore a suit and a tie. He carried a shiny briefcase. His gray eyes were cold behind his horn-rimmed glasses, but it was his frown that made Hayley shiver.

"That's Mr. Penwick," murmured Hayley's best friend, Olivia. "He's on the school board. My mother sold him a house." Mrs. Watson was a real estate agent. She knew practically everyone in town.

The man was talking to Ms. Lyons in a loud voice. "We've got to save money!" he boomed. "I'll bet the kids won't even notice the cutbacks."

The third graders tiptoed past the principal. Ms. Lyons nodded at them approvingly. But as soon as they rounded the corner, Hayley tugged on Olivia's sleeve. "Cutbacks? What cutbacks? What's Mr. Penwick mean?" she whispered.

"No field trips." Olivia shook her head sadly.

"No art classes," said Skeeter. "No soccer team. PE only once a week."

"They can't do that!" said Hayley.

"Mr. Penwick can," said Olivia. "And—to save electricity—he made us have three weeks of winter break instead of two!"

"Well, that's a good thing!" said Skeeter.

They stopped talking when they reached the music room. Something was different! There were the usual rows of chairs. The same old music stands. The same old posters on the walls. But instead of Mrs. Smith, the old music teacher, someone new stood in front of the classroom. A tall African American man in a bright red vest and a yellow bow tie. He smiled broadly at the kids.

"Good morning!" he said. "I'm your new music teacher. My name is Mr. Yaeger. But you can call me Mr. Y."

"Why not?" yelled Skeeter, flopping down into one of the chairs. He laughed at his own joke.

With his shaved head, goatee, and earring, Mr. Y was a big change from Mrs. Beatrice Smith. Mrs. Smith had been the Bridgewater music teacher ever since Hayley was in kindergarten. Mrs. Smith had played an ancient record player. She had sung in a high, quavery voice. All the kids had loved her. Well, most of the kids. Make that some of the kids. She retired last spring. Hayley had eaten cupcakes at her retirement party.

Now, Mr. Y was in charge of the music room.

Mr. Y was still talking. Hayley stopped daydreaming and focused. Just like Dad always told her: "Focus, Hayley. Pay attention."

"Talent show," Mr. Y continued. "Anyone can sign up. The show will be December fifth. I'm telling you now, even though it's only September, so you'll have time to prepare."

A talent show! Mrs. Smith had never done anything cool like that!

"I'll help anyone polish up his or her act," Mr. Yaeger added. "Just let me know."

"I can juggle!" shouted Robin.

"Michelle and I can do double Dutch jump rope!" said Zelda. Michelle nodded.

"How about skateboard stunts?" called Skeeter.

"Sorry, no skateboards. We don't have room on the stage to perform stunts safely," said Mr. Y.

"Rats!"

"You can do a solo act or work in groups. You can act out skits. You can sing, dance, or play an instrument."

"I do stand-up comedy," said Devon.

"As long as it's clean!" said Mr. Y. "This is a family show!" Everyone laughed.

Lupe didn't say anything. But then, she never did. She came from Mexico. She'd said *"buenos días"* to Mrs. McCann and had not said anything since.

When music was over, the class lined up. Mr. Y didn't make them line up by height. But Hayley got at the end anyway. She pulled Olivia into line in front of her.

"I'm going to dance for my talent," said Olivia. "Ballet." She twirled gracefully around on her tiptoes. She'd been adopted from China when she was a baby. She went to Chinese Culture Club every Thursday in addition to ballet.

Skeeter slid in front of them. "I'll bet I can burp 'The Star-Spangled Banner,'" he said. He belched loudly just to practice.

"I'm going to sign up too!" said Hayley.

"But Hayley, you don't have any talent," Skeeter pointed out. "You can't sing on key. You flunked out of ballet. Your jokes stink. And you can't juggle," he added.

"That's mean!" said Olivia.

Skeeter raised his eyebrows in surprise. "Whaaat? What'd I say?" he asked.

Hayley knew Skeeter didn't intend to be mean. But his wisecracks still stung. Was Skeeter right? Was she a no-talent shrimp? She picked at a scab on her elbow.

"I must have some talent," she said at last. "Mr. Y says everyone does. Maybe I just need to find mine!"

Hidden talent. Hayley thought about that as she followed the line back to the third grade room. Maybe her talent was like treasure in a pirate chest. Waiting to be discovered. But what could that talent be?

2

Go-Away-Hayley

All weekend Hayley tried to discover her hidden talent. Ventriloquist? No. Tightrope walker? No again.

Stilt walker! That was it!

Definitely not stilt walker, she thought later, putting an ice pack on her bruised knee.

She *could* hang a spoon from her nose. Her family thought it was hilarious. It brought down the house every Thanksgiving. But it wouldn't be a good act for a talent show.

Maybe she was an animal trainer! Hayley had two hamster sisters that lived in a glass tank in her room. Mango and Tango. They had apricot-colored fur. They were round and furry and warm. They munched on carrot sticks and kibbles. But they could not seem to learn any tricks.

"Mango," said Hayley, tapping on the glass. "Are you listening?" Mango stopped nibbling her kibbles.

"When I blow the whistle, jump through the hoop." Hayley had made a hoop out of chenille stems. She blew the whistle, but Mango just sat there. Hayley sighed. Tango wasn't any better. Clearly, Hayley wasn't a star animal trainer.

"Looky!" A shout came from the hall. Hayley's little sister, Tilly, burst in. She wore pink footie pajamas. A red cape. A purple eye mask.

"Super Tilly!" she yelled, scrambling up Hayley's unmade bed. She waved her arms around like a windmill. "Sissy! Catch!" She jumped into Hayley's waiting arms.

Tilly grabbed for the whistle that hung around Hayley's neck. "Let me!" she demanded. Hayley gave Tilly the whistle. She'd never tell Tilly she was too little. Almost never. Well, maybe sometimes.

Hayley had not forgotten what it felt like to be too little to play.

Hayley had an older brother, Sam. And an older sister, Jennifer. They were away at college now. When Hayley was as little as Tilly, she wanted to do everything they did. Just like Tilly now.

"Let me!" she'd plead when Jennifer practiced tennis.

"Let me!" she'd yell when Sam practiced backing up the car.

But the answer was always the same. "Go away, Hayley. You're too little."

She missed her brother and sister. But she didn't miss their snubs!

So Hayley let Tilly blow the whistle until she got bored. Then Hayley wiped it off on her T-shirt and hid it in her pocket.

"I'm hungry," said Tilly. She raced down the hall to the kitchen. Hayley followed.

"Mom?" she called. "Can Tilly have a cookie? Can I?"

"Okay, hon, but just one." Mom poked her head around the corner. She was still in her scrubs from work. She dropped a kiss on the top of Hayley's head. "Daddy's making shrimp lo mein for dinner."

That word shrimp *again! Don't remind me!* thought Hayley.

Shrimp wasn't a funny nickname. Not funny at all. It hadn't been so bad when Skeeter and Hayley were both the shortest in the class and teased each other. But now that Skeeter was taller, it wasn't funny anymore. Even worse, other kids were starting to use it too. At recess yesterday, when she'd asked to join the basketball game, one of the kids had said, "If we need a garden gnome, we'll give you a call, shrimp." Now *that* was just plain mean.

But shrimp lo mein had nothing to do with rude nicknames. Shrimp lo mein was Chinese food. That sounded good. Ever since Dad got laid off from his construction job, he'd been cooking new dishes. It was part of his homework. He was going to school at the community college, in the culinary arts program. Hayley knew that was a fancy way of saying cooking school. Someday he'd be a chef, maybe, or run a restaurant. But for now he practiced at home. At least his homework was tasty. Most of the time. Make that some of the time.

Hayley looked in the cookie jar for Dad's cowboy cookies. All gone. Rats. She spotted a box of animal crackers on the top shelf. Just out of reach. She pulled a chair over and climbed up on the counter. She stretched out her hand for the box.

"I hope you aren't climbing on the counter!" Mom's voice floated down the hall.

Hayley grabbed the box and quickly scrambled down. "No, Mom," she said, feeling only slightly guilty. Well, she wasn't climbing *now*.

"Mmmm," said Tilly, munching happily. Crumbs spilled from her mouth and dusted her pj's.

Hayley finished her crackers and wandered down the hall to the big kids' rooms. She looked at Sam's shelf of trophies: football, marching band, basketball, baseball, science club.

She looked at Jennifer's wall of blue ribbons: horseback riding, tennis, homecoming queen, valedictorian. Her heart swelled with pride. They were talented, all right. Shining stars. Compared to them, Hayley sometimes felt invisible.

Behind her, Tilly raced down the hall in her cape, pretending to fly. Mom came out of the laundry room.

"Isn't she adorable?" said Mom. She scooped Tilly up in a hug. "Cute as a bug!"

Jennifer and Sam were bright, shining stars. And Tilly was as cute as a bug. *Where does that leave me?*

3

Yard Sale Saturday

"Who wants to go to a yard sale?" called Dad.

It was the last Saturday in September. The sky was blue, with just a few puffy clouds. The sun shone. T-shirt weather. The kind of day anything could happen.

"I do!" yelled Hayley.

"Me too! Me too!" yelled Tilly.

Copycat, thought Hayley, as she sprinted upstairs to find her piggy bank.

Hayley found her pink china pig under a pile of dirty clothes. She unplugged the rubber stopper on the bottom of the pig and shook out the coins. She pried out the wadded-up dollar bills with her pinky. Four dollars. Eleven cents. Earned by picking up pop cans from the side of the road. Hoarded for weeks. That didn't seem like much. Would it be enough for something good?

Her family waited in the garage. Dad ruffled Hayley's wild curls. "Nothing I like better than a day out with my redheads!" he said. Hayley's hair glowed copper, like Mom's and Tilly's.

"You're just jealous!" said Hayley, strapping on her bike helmet. She knew Dad didn't mind her teasing him about the bald spot he covered with a baseball cap.

"Someday, I'll cover it with a chef's toque!" Dad replied.

"If you find something you like, don't forget to bargain," reminded Mom as they climbed on their bikes.

Hayley loved yard sales. Once she had bought a box of colored chalk for a dime. She and Olivia had drawn pictures all over the sidewalk in front of her house. The picture had stayed there until it rained.

Another time she'd bought an old red wagon for two dollars. Never mind that it only had three wheels. She had hauled it up to her room and propped it up on a brick. Now it held her stuffed animals. But she didn't like to bargain. It was hard to get over her shyness enough to ask for a lower price.

Hayley pressed down on the pedals. Dad took the lead, with Tilly strapped in the bike trailer behind him. Hayley followed, and Mom brought up the end.

"I'm the cow's tail!" Mom called, waving. Mom was a vet tech at the veterinarian's office. Dad said he was the bread baker, but Mom was the bread winner.

They rode down the block. Dad signaled for a left turn. They all glided around the corner. The yard sale was about two miles from the house. Hayley's face

was hot by the time they got there. She took off her helmet and ran her hands through her sweaty hair. It had to be the hottest day of the whole fall.

The yard sale beckoned like Aladdin's cave. Hidden treasures! Mounds of clothes. Heaps of toys. Boxes of books.

Mom headed for the toddler clothes. Dad headed for the kitchen items. Tilly headed for an old potty chair. "Not that!" said Dad, scooping her up just in time.

Hayley spotted an old TV in the corner. Cool! She

looked at the price. Fifty dollars. Too much. Not even bargaining could make that work!

A large woman in a bright orange muumuu came over. "Help you find something?" she asked. Her brown hair was in a bun. She wore a pair of glittery glasses shoved up on the top of her hair.

Hayley shook her head. "Just looking." She dug through the boxes, piles, and bins but came up empty-handed.

"I found three pairs of pants in Tilly's size!" said Mom. "Hayley, come here a minute." Mom held up a pair of jeans, matching them to Hayley's waist. They were really cute, with embroidered butterflies on the pockets. "Nearly new!" said Mom happily, adding them to her pile.

"Look at this!" said Dad. He held up a big soup kettle. "Copper bottom. They don't make 'em like this anymore!" He added a wooden soup spoon and a lid.

Even Tilly found something. She held up a stuffed pink rabbit with one blue eye. "Bun-Bun!" she declared happily.

"Time to go," said Dad. "I have to get home and start my homework. I'm making *lengua de res*!"

"What's that?" asked Hayley.

"Beef tongue," said Mom. She folded the jeans and put them into the trailer.

"Ick!" said Hayley.

"You'll like it," Dad promised. He loaded Tilly into the trailer and handed her the soup kettle.

"We can't go yet!" cried Hayley. She couldn't make up her mind. Should she get the jar of old buttons? Or the half-used tablet of drawing paper? Neither one seemed like much of a deal. And then she saw something she hadn't seen before.

It was in a dark corner on top of a dusty old refrigerator. She could just see the handle sticking out. She jumped, but she couldn't reach. Too short, again!

"Need a hand, honey?" asked the lady in the orange dress. Hayley nodded, and the lady took it down and handed it to her.

It looked like a miniature guitar. Brown wood, with a palm tree and a hula girl stenciled on the front. Curly script read, "Souvenir of Hawaii." Hayley ran her fingers lightly across the strings. They twanged unpleasantly.

She wanted to ask the price but felt too shy. "How much?" she finally squeaked.

The lady put her cat's-eye glasses down on her nose. She took the instrument and blew off the dust. "Oh, that old thing, Gramps's ukulele. Let's see now. How's five dollars sound?"

Hayley felt her face fall. Five dollars! Too much. She remembered Mom's advice about bargaining. The lady in the orange dress was still looking at her. She couldn't possibly ask for a lower price. But, oh! She wanted the ukulele more than anything.

She looked around for Mom and Dad for help, but they were already in the driveway. Could she do it herself? Could she bargain? She took a deep, steadying breath. "Well, I don't know," she said. "It's awfully old. It might not work anymore."

"Four-fifty," said the woman, with a smile.

Hayley touched the money in her pocket. "Four dollars?" she asked.

"Done!" said the woman. She took the money and handed Hayley the ukulele. The ukulele was hers! That hadn't been so hard after all.

Hayley wrapped the uke in the jeans Mom had found. She tucked the bundle into Dad's new soup kettle. Tilly put Bun-Bun on top and held the whole thing on her lap in the bike trailer. They rode their bikes home like they were in a parade.

Dad was pleased because he had saved money and had a soup kettle big enough to cook a meal with plenty of leftovers.

Mom was pleased because she'd saved clothes from the landfill.

Tilly was pleased because the bunny was pink, her favorite color.

But Hayley chewed her lower lip. She only had eleven cents left now. And for what? The uke was old. It was dusty. It twanged.

Was it a genuine hidden treasure? Or a waste of money?

4

Ruby and Her Ragtime Rascals

"What did you buy?" asked Dad when they got home. Dad took the soup kettle from Tilly, unfastened her seat belt, and picked her out of the bike trailer. "I didn't have a chance to look at it."

Hayley pulled the ukulele out of the kettle.

"You spent your hard-earned money on this?" said Mom doubtfully. She plucked the strings. *Twang!*

But Dad was more encouraging. "A ukulele!" he said. "Say, I think one of your great-great-aunts played the ukulele in a band of some kind. We've got a photo someplace."

"A band? Really?" said Hayley. Maybe the uke wasn't a waste of money after all. "Show me the picture."

But first there was dinner to make. *Lengua de res* turned out to be pretty tasty, even if it was tongue. And then the kitchen had to be cleaned up. Then it was time to bathe Tilly and time for Hayley to study her spelling words. Then it was time for Hayley's bath, and then storytime, and finally bedtime. And somehow, the ukulele stayed in the garage, forgotten.

Hayley didn't remember the uke again until Monday night. After dinner, Dad pulled the family photo album off the shelf. He sat on the couch. Hayley curled up next to him. She liked looking through the old black photo album at the old cars and old clothes and funny haircuts. Dad told good stories about the people of long ago.

"Here it is," he said, pointing to a faded black-and-white photograph. "Great-great Aunt Ruby." A 1920s flapper posed for the camera, holding a ukulele. Ruby wore a short dress and a hat that covered most of her short hair. A long beaded necklace hung almost to her knees. Four young men with slicked-back hair surrounded her. They also held ukuleles—some big, some small.

"Ruby and Her Ragtime Rascals," said Dad. "They traveled all around the country playing music."

Hayley read the caption. "*Ain't she sweet? Ruby, 1926.*" She noticed something else. Ruby wore a leg brace. "What's that?" asked Hayley. "Did she break her leg?"

"Disabled by polio," said Dad. "She got the disease as a young girl."

"She performed anyway? Wow. She must have been talented."

"And determined," said Dad. "In those days, people with disabilities were sometimes treated as if they were invisible. But that didn't stop Ruby."

Hayley studied the photo. In spite of the leg brace, Ruby was smiling.

"I want to do that too," said Hayley. She ran to the garage. Where had she put that ukulele? She finally found it under her bicycle helmet.

She raced back inside. She cradled the ukulele in her arms and spun around the room, singing loudly. Tilly grabbed her stuffed, one-eyed bunny and twirled too. Hayley came to a stop in front of her parents.

"I have a great idea!" she exclaimed. "I'll play the ukulele in the school talent show! Ukulele Hayley and Her Ragtime Rascals! That can be my hidden talent!"

Mom smiled. "Some of your plans don't work out," she said gently. "Remember when you wanted to be in the summer camp skit?"

Hayley shuddered. "Don't remind me." She had learned her lines, rehearsed, even made her costume. But when it had come time to go onstage, she'd frozen. Olivia had to take her place.

"That was way back in first grade!" she pointed out. "I'm much braver now."

"First, you have to how learn to play." Dad patted the top of her head. "If you put half as much energy into learning to play as you do making big plans, you'll have no problem!"

At least they didn't say she was too little. *Never mind,* thought Hayley. *If Ruby could do it, so can I.*

5

On Top of Spaghetti

Hayley took the uke to school, wrapped in a bath towel and buried in her backpack. She wanted to show it to Mr. Y. If only she could work up the courage to talk to him. He was still new, practically a stranger. Maybe Olivia or Skeeter could come with her. They never seemed to be afraid of anything!

Skeeter was in the hall, trying to walk on his hands. "I'm going to juggle with my feet for the talent show!" he said.

"What happened to burping 'The Star-Spangled Banner'?" asked Hayley.

Skeeter flopped over and stood up. "Couldn't hit the high notes." He eyed the bump in her backpack. "What's that?"

"That's for me to know and you to find out!" Hayley replied, proud of her snappy comeback. Really, Skeeter was so annoying. Following her around and bugging her. As bad as Tilly!

She begged her friends to come with her, but Olivia had Chinese Culture Club and Skeeter had to stand by the wall for jumping off the swings. So at lunch recess, Hayley got out the uke. She took it down the hall to the music room. Mr. Y was at his desk, eating a sandwich. Hayley took a deep breath. *I can do this,* she thought.

"Hey!" said Mr. Y. "A vintage uke." Hayley told him how she'd found it and bargained for it.

"Can you teach me to play?" she asked shyly. "Can I be in the talent show? Can we start a ukulele band at school?"

"Not so fast!" Mr. Y laughed. "I can get you started playing. But you'll have to practice every day if you want to be in the talent show. That's only two months away. As far as starting a band—lots of schools have uke bands. But I'm pretty busy teaching band. And choir. And general music. Plus the talent show and winter concert coming up." He scratched his goatee thoughtfully. "Does anyone else play the uke?"

Hayley shook her head. "I don't know."

Mr. Y smiled. "First things first, then. Let's get you started. We need to tune. Because you can tune a uke, but you can't tuna fish!" Hayley laughed. She liked Mr. Y's jokes. Really, talking to him wasn't so scary after all.

Mr. Y wiped the dust away with a soft cloth. "Not bad," he said. "Solid wood. You paid four bucks? You got a good deal."

Hayley glowed. She hadn't wasted her money after all.

Mr. Y clamped a small gadget on to the top of the uke. "This is a digital tuner," he said. "You can buy one at a music store. Each string is tuned to a different note." He plucked each string and twisted the tuning pegs until the light turned green.

Mr. Y strummed the uke softly. A chord rang out. It sounded like music now, not *plunk, plunk, twang.*

"Good cooks eat a lot," Mr. Y said.

"What?" said Hayley, surprised. What did cooking have to do with playing the ukulele?

"That's how you remember the tuning," Mr. Y said, laughing. He plucked the strings one at a time. "Each string has a name. This is the G string. *Good.* C. *Cooks.* E. *Eat.* A. *A lot.* Now you need to learn some chords. Once you learn a few chords, you can play a lot of songs."

Mr. Yaeger strummed a few chords and then played "On Top of Spaghetti," a song the third graders sang in class. She itched to try it for herself. She held out her hands and Mr. Y handed her the uke.

"Put your left thumb behind the neck," he instructed. "Curl your fingers over the fretboard. Press the strings down with your fingers. Like this." He showed her how to strum across the strings with the index finger of her right hand.

"Here's how you play a C chord," he said. He put the third finger of her left hand on the first string of the third fret. Then he showed her an F chord and a G chord.

"Practice those three chords and you can play hundreds of songs," he told her. "Here's a song sheet

with the chords. It will show you when to change chords." He handed her a piece of paper with the words to "On Top of Spaghetti" on it. Above the lyrics were the chord symbols—C, F, G.

Slowly, Hayley stumbled through the song. When she was done, she grinned. "I can do this!" she cried.

Mr. Y laughed. "Of course you can!"

The bell rang. Lunch recess was over. Time to go back to Mrs. McCann's class. Hayley floated out of the music room on a cloud, still strumming. The strings quivered under her fingers. She loved the shivery feel.

"Hayley!" Mr. Y waved from the door. "I found a

ukulele book you can borrow." He handed her a small booklet. "This'll help you get started. Good luck!"

As she left the room, she saw Mr. Penwick, the school board member, in the hall. He carried his briefcase, as usual. A short, dark-haired woman stood next to him, arguing. Hayley couldn't hear the woman, but Mr. Penwick's loud voice echoed down the hall.

"Money doesn't grow on trees!" he insisted.

That's funny, thought Hayley. *That's what Dad always says.*

Hayley had to walk past him to get to class. She tried to make herself small and sneak by. Mr. Penwick glared in her direction, but she could tell he didn't really see her. He was intent on making his point. He pounded his fist into his palm. "More cuts are absolutely necessary!"

6

Easier Said Than Done

Easier said than done. That's what Dad always said when one of his recipes didn't work out. Learning to play the ukulele was just like that—easier said than done.

At first, Hayley's fingers got stiff and sore. It was too hard! When she got discouraged, she brought out the family album and flipped to Ruby's picture. Her leg brace. Her smile. You could see Ruby wasn't the kind of person who gave up easily.

I have to do this, thought Hayley. *Am I a no-talent shrimp, or a shining star?*

So Hayley practiced every day. She studied the ukulele book. She watched videos on YouTube too. Sometimes it was hard, but there was something satisfying about getting music out of that little wooden box. Hayley couldn't seem to put it down.

"Come help me with my magic act for the talent

show," said Skeeter after school one day. "I'm going to saw a lady in half. You can be the lady."

"I thought you were going to juggle with your feet," said Hayley.

"I was, but my mom won't let me have any more eggs."

Hayley rolled her eyes. "No thanks. I'd rather play my uke."

"Spoilsport," said Skeeter. But he grinned, so she knew he wasn't mad.

Hayley played when she was supposed to be doing homework. She played when she was supposed to be doing chores. She even played in bed when she was supposed to be sleeping, muffling the sound with her blankets.

"I've never seen you so determined!" said Dad.

But then Hayley's report card came, and her parent teacher conference. "Hayley isn't working up to her potential," said Mrs. McCann. "Especially in math. She seems distracted. Is something going on at home?"

Mom and Dad looked at each other, and then at Hayley. "We'll take care of it," said Dad.

Hayley got a talking to when they got home. "No more ukulele until your homework is done. And no uke after bedtime. And you must get some fresh air and exercise every day." Mom laid down the law.

"The key is balance," said Dad.

"Like a balanced diet?" asked Hayley.

"Yes!" said Dad. "The uke is dessert."

"And math is broccoli," said Hayley sadly. She hated broccoli.

But practicing isn't always dessert, thought Hayley. *Sometimes it's oatmeal. Good for you. And you have to do it. But I'd really rather have Honey Charms!*

Even with the limits, she could soon play "Happy Birthday" for Tilly's third birthday in October. Dad made cherry cupcakes with pink frosting flowers. Hayley strummed her uke and everyone sang. Tilly banged along with her spoon. She had frosting on her nose and a bow from one of her packages stuck in her hair. Cute as a bug!

Pretty soon Hayley could switch chords without looking at her fingers. By Halloween, she could play "Skip to My Lou" and "Down in the Valley," and a bunch of other songs.

She played for Mom and Dad. She played for Mango and Tango, though they slept right through it. But Tilly was her best audience. Tilly never got tired of hearing Hayley play. She'd put on her ballet tutu and her princess crown. "Play the 'lele!" she'd demand. Then she'd twirl and dance while Hayley played.

Hayley even found the courage to play for Mr. Y. He said she was coming along nicely and showed her some new chords. Encouraged by his praise, she played in the hall at lunch recess for Skeeter and Olivia, and anyone else who came by. Skeeter said he was going to get a uke too, but then he forgot. That was Skeeter!

"I might get one too," said Olivia, thoughtfully. "I wonder if they come in pink." But somehow, between ballet and Chinese Club, she never got around to it.

By Thanksgiving, Hayley could play a lot of three-chord songs. But she wanted to play something really cool for the talent show. Something new. Something different. Something amazing! Something to prove she wasn't a no-talent shrimp any longer.

"You need a showstopper," said Dad. He was in the kitchen, taking a pan of blondies out of the oven. Hayley closed her eyes and sniffed. Yum! She loved Dad's brown sugar brownies.

"What's a showstopper, Dad?" she asked. She licked her finger and rubbed it over the counter to pick up crumbs.

"A song that will astonish everyone. Make them stop in their tracks and open their mouths in surprise!" Dad demonstrated as he cut into the blondies. He handed Hayley a chunk. "Standing ovations! Cheers! Applause! Hayley brings down the house!" He swept his oven mitt toward her with a flourish.

A smile spread across her face. "Yes!" she said. "That's what I need. A showstopper!"

December came, but Hayley couldn't decide what would be her showstopper. She sat on the front porch swing. It was chilly, and Hayley was bundled up in her coat. She strummed her uke. She rocked back and forth in time to her music.

Of all the chords she was learning, D7 was the hardest. She couldn't squeeze all of her fingers into that small space and still press hard enough to make the strings sound. *Buzz!* That was the only sound she could get.

"Rats!" she grumbled.

"You're doing it all wrong," said a voice. Hayley looked up. Curtis Randall stood on the sidewalk. Curtis was a fifth grader. He'd just moved in down the street. Hayley didn't know him well, and she didn't want to. Curtis was always scowling. Olivia said he was cute, but Hayley thought he looked like a growly old bear.

"What do you mean?" she asked. "I'm doing it like the book says."

Curtis clomped up the steps and held out his hand.

"Do you know how to play?" Hayley asked. She handed the uke over. Curtis grunted. He tucked the uke under his arm and strummed. He frowned and fiddled with the tuning pegs. Then he launched into a tune Hayley had heard on the radio. The song had about a zillion chords. Curtis's fingers flew over the strings. He didn't sing, but he didn't have to. The melody was in the music.

Hayley's mouth dropped open. Now *that* was a showstopper. "Wow," she said. "Where'd you learn to play like that?"

Curtis ignored her. "There's an easier way to play

D7," he told her. "Put two fingers here, like this. You can switch to the other chord when your fingers get stronger." He handed the uke back. "That's how we do it in Hawaii." He started down the stairs.

"But wait!" cried Hayley. "You've been to Hawaii?

How did you learn to play so well? Want to start a band? We could be in the talent show together!"

Curtis turned his head toward her. "No, I don't want to play with you. Why would I want to play with a little kid?" He clomped back down the stairs and slouched away, hands in his pockets.

Hayley stuck her tongue out at his back. Too little! She never wanted to hear that again!

7

Talent Show

The day of the talent show, Hayley's stomach fluttered like a flock of baby birds. Was this how Ruby felt before a performance with her Ragtime Rascals?

Mom had helped Hayley make her costume. Black-and-white saddle shoes, a poodle skirt, blouse, and a scarf tied around her neck. Her hair, as usual, was a wild mop of red curls. She'd tried to pull it back in a ponytail, but it was coming loose already. Couldn't do anything about that!

There had been some rumors that the talent show would have to be canceled due to cutbacks. But somehow it had worked out, and now Hayley waited backstage, softly strumming her uke.

She'd practiced a lot. At the talent show tryouts, Mr. Y had given her a thumbs-up and told her that she was in. Dad and Mom had cheered.

"You'll bring the house down!" said Dad.

"What's that mean?" asked Tilly, anxiously looking at the ceiling. Mom laughed and hugged her.

"It means your big sis is going to be a star!"

Now Hayley peeked through the curtains to the front of the stage. There were a lot of acts. She watched Skeeter pull a rabbit out of a hat—or try to. The rabbit was a stuffed animal, and he dropped it twice before he finished. Being Skeeter, he didn't mind when the audience laughed. He bowed with a big flourish and dropped the rabbit again. This time, even Skeeter laughed.

Olivia was next. She wore a fluffy tutu and pink satin shoes. Hayley thought she twirled as gracefully as a real ballerina. Then two fifth grade girls danced to a popular song. Some fourth graders performed a silly skit. A kindergartener tried to recite a poem, got scared, and had to be helped off the stage by his teacher.

Finally, the MC announced Hayley. She walked out to the front of the stage. She stood in front of the mic the way Mr. Y told her to.

She looked out into the gym. All the kids in the school looked back. Her stomach flopped. Her knees knocked. Her head spun. Why had she ever thought this would be fun? She wanted to crawl back in bed. Forget the whole thing. Be little Hayley, the shrimp, again.

She spotted Mr. Penwick at the back of the auditorium. He leaned against the wall, frowning. His ever-present briefcase was at his feet and his arms were crossed. *Him again!* thought Hayley. *What's he doing here?*

Then the spotlight came on. She took a deep breath, and suddenly all of her butterflies flew away. She grinned. She tossed her head, making her curls dance. Bring it on! She was ready!

She tucked her uke under her arm and strummed the first chord. "*One, two, three o'clock!*" she sang, "*Four o'clock rock!*" She played an old rock 'n' roll song from the fifties. She finished by swinging her

arm in a big circle like a guitar hero. Just the way she'd practiced.

The gym erupted with applause and cheers. She was a shining star!

The talent show made Hayley a celebrity. Well, not a celebrity exactly, but at least famous. Maybe not famous. Make that sort of well-known.

Kids kept coming up and telling her how cool she was. "Can we join your band?" they asked.

"But I don't have a band," she said.

"Start one," Skeeter advised.

"Okay," said Hayley. "Anyone who wants to be in my band, get a ukulele, and I'll teach you to play."

On Monday, Michelle, Justin, and Robin waited for her in the hall. They all had ukuleles. Hayley tuned their ukes. She showed them how to play a C chord. They were all banging away when Mrs. McCann opened the classroom door. She peered into the hall. She frowned when she saw the four kids. "What's going on?" she asked.

"I'm starting a band," said Hayley. "A uke band."

Mrs. McCann gave a faint smile. "Okay, but you can't rehearse here. I have a meeting. Try the lunchroom." They moved down to the lunchroom and practiced until the bell rang.

On Tuesday six kids with ukes waited for Hayley in the lunchroom. Zelda, Anna, and Linden had joined Michelle, Justin, and Robin.

Hayley tuned all six ukuleles and told everyone

they should get digital tuners. "Buy one at the music store," she said. Then she showed the G chord to go with the C chord and taught the kids to play "Skip to My Lou."

Wednesday Skeeter showed up too. He carried a shiny new green ukulele. The six kids showed up again, so with Skeeter and Hayley, now there were eight. They learned the F chord and played "On Top of Spaghetti."

Thursday Olivia brought a purple uke to school. "The music store was out of pink ukes," she said. "But I painted my nails to match." She showed Hayley her purple fingernails.

Olivia made nine. Nine kids in Hayley's uke band! They sat on top of the lunchroom tables. They played and sang with enthusiasm, if not tunefulness.

Curtis walked past the open door. He stopped when he heard them banging out "Twinkle, Twinkle, Little Star." He rolled his eyes as if he couldn't believe his ears and walked away.

Hayley nudged Olivia. "I wish he'd join the band. He's really good. He could teach us a lot, I bet."

"I wish he'd join too," said Olivia. "I think he's cute." She giggled.

The next week ten kids sat on top of the tables in the lunchroom. Hayley was teaching "The Ants Go Marching Two by Two."

Mr. Harvey, the janitor, came over. "You can't play here anymore," he told Hayley. "I've got five tables to set up for breakfast. Then I've got to take them down, mop, and set up for the first lunch." He shook his head. "Ever since they let Bob go, I have to do both jobs. Not enough hours in the day!"

"But where are we going to practice?" asked Hayley. "We can't use Mrs. McCann's room. The gym is full of PE kids. And the librarian will never let us play in the library." She giggled, thinking of the noise.

Mr. Harvey shook his head. The cutbacks made everyone grumpy. "Not my problem. Go outside." It was too cold to practice outside, so the group played in the hall.

A few days later, Hayley saw Curtis in the hall alone. He was playing a uke. It wasn't colorful. It didn't have a palm tree and a hula girl. It was the color of brown sugar and had dark stripes along the sides. It was bigger too, and louder. The notes rang out clear and clean. He sounded as good as the Hawaiian guy on YouTube.

"Wow," said Hayley. "Come play with us. You can be the star."

Curtis didn't answer. He didn't even look at her. He just tucked his uke under his arm and walked away. *What's up with him?* she wondered.

Now that she was paying attention, Hayley noticed that Curtis was always alone. He didn't seem to have any friends, not even fifth graders. At recess he leaned against the wall of the school, strumming. Just Curtis and his uke.

Pretty soon, Hayley forgot all about Curtis. She had her hands full with her band. One morning, ten kids sat in the hall singing "The Blue-Tailed Fly."

Ms. Lyons, the principal, came over. "What's going on here?" she asked.

"It's my band. A ukulele band. I'm teaching everyone how to play," said Hayley.

Ms. Lyons shook her head. "Hayley, as much as I admire your initiative, we can't have an unauthorized group meeting in the hallway."

"Why not?" asked Hayley, surprising herself. Go-Away-Hayley would have backed down. Ukulele Hayley did not. Olivia gasped. Skeeter giggled. Even Ms. Lyons seemed taken aback.

But she didn't give up. "Because it causes problems with noise and traffic flow." Ms. Lyons folded her arms.

"We can play quieter!" said Hayley.

"No," said Ms. Lyons.

"We can sit like this." Hayley scooted up next to the wall. "Then we won't take up any room." She smiled at Ms. Lyons—her nicest, most reasonable smile.

Ms. Lyons didn't give in. "No."

"What about the chess club? And the science club? They have meetings."

"If you want this group to be a club, you'll need a teacher to sponsor you, and a designated, supervised place to meet," Ms. Lyons said. "Not in the hallway. Now, put the ukuleles away. Go outside and get some exercise." With that, she walked away, her high heels snapping like castanets.

You Can't Tuna Fish

The uke kids went outside. Only Skeeter, Olivia, and Hayley were left.

"Wow, Hayley. You really stood up for us," said Skeeter.

"But it didn't do any good," Hayley said, sadly.

"I guess that's the end of our band," said Skeeter. "Too bad. I was just starting to get the hang of it."

"It isn't fair," said Olivia. "They let the chess club meet, and the science club. Even the Chinese Culture Club!"

"Maybe if we were a *club*, instead of a *band*...," began Hayley.

"You heard Ms. Lyons," Skeeter interrupted. "We need a sponsor. And a place to meet."

"Who can we get to sponsor us? Mr. Benniger, the assistant principal, used to organize the clubs, but now he's gone too." Olivia made a face. "All these cuts. It isn't fair."

"Let's ask Mr. Y!" said Hayley. "He's the music teacher. He could sponsor us!" Hayley wasn't scared to talk to Mr. Y anymore. He'd become a good friend. They trooped down to the music room to ask him.

Mr. Y listened. He scratched his head. "I'd love to help," he said. "But I'm swamped. I can't sneak one more thing into my schedule."

Hayley made puppy dog eyes at him. Skeeter got down on his knees like he was praying. Olivia smiled her most adorable smile.

Mr. Y laughed. "Far be it from me to squelch budding musicians!" he said. "Okay. But here's the deal. The ukulele club will be open to anyone in the school who wants to join. Everyone must have a signed permission slip and a contract agreeing to practice at home. I'll supply those. Hayley, you are in charge. When you've taught the group everything you know, I'll take over. If we are going to have a band—it must be a *good* band. No slackers. Got that?" They nodded.

In charge! Hayley glowed all the way home. She wasn't too little. She was *in charge!*

On Monday Hayley waited in the office to make her announcement. She noticed Curtis slouched in one of the chairs outside Ms. Lyons's office. *Waiting to see the principal,* she thought. *I wonder why he's in trouble?*

Then she forgot about him. She was about to talk on the intercom! She had begged Olivia to do it instead, but Olivia refused.

"You can do this, Hayley," she said.

So now, here she was—Little Hayley—about to talk to the whole entire school! She had to swallow twice before the words came out.

"Announcing a new club at school! The Ukulele Club!" She stopped to take a deep breath. Talking over the intercom wasn't so bad. Not as scary as the talent show, anyway. At least no one was looking at her! "If you want to join, see Mr. Y or Hayley Godwin to sign up. We will meet on Tuesdays and Thursdays at lunch recess in the music room. Bring your own ukulele." Her voice only cracked once.

When she got back to class, everyone cheered. Olivia beamed at her. Skeeter slapped her on the back. Mrs. McCann gave her a big smile. Even Lupe smiled shyly.

Later that morning, Mrs. McCann called Hayley up to her desk. The other kids were bent over their math books. *Uh-oh,* thought Hayley. *What did I do now?*

But she wasn't in trouble. "I'd like you to do me a favor," Mrs. McCann said.

"Okay," said Hayley.

"I'd like you to take Lupe to your ukulele club," said Mrs. McCann.

Hayley looked over at Lupe. She was not doing math. She was staring into space. "Does she want to join?" asked Hayley. She didn't want to force anyone.

Mrs. McCann lowered her voice. "I think she's too shy to ask," she said gently. "Belonging to a club would help her make friends. Give her a chance to improve her English."

Hayley could sympathize with being shy. She'd been shy herself before learning to play the ukulele. And she liked Lupe. Well, she probably liked Lupe. Come to think of it, she didn't know whether she liked Lupe or not. Lupe never said a word. "Does she have a uke?" Hayley asked.

"Don't worry about that," said Mrs. McCann firmly. "I'll see that she gets one."

The first meeting of the Ukulele Club was Tuesday. The usual ten kids, plus Lupe, showed up in the music room.

And a few other kids. Make that a lot of other kids! Every chair was full. There were kids in chairs, kids on risers, and even kids sitting on the floor. Hayley counted fifteen. Fifteen kids! And not just third graders, either. Kindergarteners. Second graders. Fourth—even fifth graders!

But not Curtis. Hayley was disappointed. It would really be something to have a great player like Curtis in their band.

Hayley knew some of the kids, but not all. Most of the kids carried a ukulele. Pink, yellow, green, blue. A rainbow of colors. Lupe had a brand-new orange uke, a loan from Mrs. McCann.

But no one else has a uke with a palm tree and a hula girl, thought Hayley. *Mine is one of a kind. Like me!*

A few kids didn't have ukes. "But I'm going to get one! As soon as I get my allowance!" said Jason.

"Me too!" said the others. "Please let us stay?"

Hayley shrugged. "Okay."

"Whew!" said Mr. Y when he saw all the kids. He handed out permission slips and contracts. "Hayley, do you think you can handle this group?"

Hayley took a deep breath. Could she? Little Hayley? The shrimp? She grinned. "No problem-o, Mr. Y!" she said, snapping a salute.

The noise was terrific. Everyone was talking or singing or trying to play. The ukes twanged like a cat fight. Hayley stood on a riser. She put her hands on her hips. She put on her outside voice, just like Mrs. McCann did when the third grade got rowdy.

"QUIET!" she roared. And everyone was.

Not all of the kids had tuners, so Mr. Y taught the club how to tune without one. First, he told everyone the names of the strings. Then, he plucked the C string. Everyone plucked their C strings. Finally, Mr. Y showed how to turn the tuning peg until the pitch matched.

"You can tune a uke...," he said.

"I know! I know!" said Hayley. "But you can't tuna fish!"

At last everyone was more or less in tune.

"You can remember the notes by singing 'My Dog Has Fleas'," said Mr. Y.

"I thought it was Good Cooks Eat A lot," said Hayley, puzzled.

"That gives you the names of the strings—GCEA. 'My Dog Has Fleas' gives you the melody." He plucked each string on Hayley's uke and had the group sing along.

"I'd better get a uke too," said Mr. Y, scratching his goatee. "Maybe a red one to match my vest!"

Tuning thirteen ukes took a long time. There was only enough time left for Hayley to teach everyone the C chord. The whole group strummed along with Hayley. Then the recess bell rang, and the first meeting was over.

"Don't forget to practice!" Hayley yelled, as the kids rushed out. "On Thursday we will learn the G chord!"

On Thursday the group learned G. Mr. Y handed

out song sheets. The chords were written above the words.

"This is the start of our club songbook," he told them. "Keep all the song sheets in a binder. Every week we'll add a few new songs."

Hayley led "Skip to My Lou" and "Buffalo Gals." And that was the end of the second meeting.

But next week was winter vacation. Three weeks with no school. As Hayley walked to the school bus, she wondered, *Will anyone still want to be in the Ukulele Club after vacation? Or will everyone forget all about it?*

BUGs

She didn't need to worry. On Monday after vacation, eight more kids showed up with ukuleles. Christmas and Hanukkah presents. Now there were twenty-three kids in the ukulele club!

"The school is full of kids who want to play," Hayley told her parents at dinner. They were having chicken tikka masala, an Indian dish Dad was working on. They'd had it three times so far this week, but this was the best.

"Crawling out of the woodwork," said Dad. He passed Hayley the salad.

Hayley laughed at the image. "Like ants or bugs or something." She speared a tomato with her fork.

"Bugs!" said Mom. "That should be the name for your club—Bridgewater Ukulele Group! BUGs!"

At the next meeting, Hayley suggested the name.

"We should be The Soggy Froggy Uke Band," said Skeeter.

"No!" yelled Josh. "We should be the Motorcycle Ninja Uke Band!" Josh was motorcycle crazy.

"Let's vote," said Hayley. The group voted. BUGs was unanimous. Almost.

Skeeter made his fingers into eyeglasses. "Call me Bugman!" he yelled.

"We should get matching T-shirts," said Olivia. She strummed a new chord.

"That's a great idea!" said Hayley. She could see the design in her mind. Ladybugs and beetles. Maybe a centipede too. All playing ukuleles.

In a few weeks, the club had a thick binder of songs they could play. And they were learning new ones all the time. At every meeting, there was something new to share.

"Look at my fingers!" said Anna. "I practiced so hard I got blisters!"

"I learned a new chord!" said Devon. He played a new chord that sounded like an old movie.

"Listen!" said Lupe. A smile lit up her face as she sang a song in Spanish. "*Mi abuelo*, my granddaddy, taught me!"

"Write out the lyrics—the words—and the chords," said Mr. Y. "So we can all learn it. We'll add it to our songbook."

Mr. Y recorded some lessons and posted the videos on the Internet. That way they could practice at home. He recorded some of their rehearsals too. Everyone liked watching themselves play.

Skeeter, Olivia, and Hayley wrote a song together. They made a video too. Then all the kids wanted to do one, so Mr. Y set up a BUGs uke channel on SchoolTube.

Olivia and Robin designed BUG shirts, based on Hayley's idea. Everyone ordered one. The group wore the red shirts when they toured the school. They stopped in each classroom and played a few songs. Soon the whole school was humming "The Lion Sleeps Tonight" and "Found a Peanut." Hayley even overheard Ms. Lyons, the principal, warbling, "It was rotten, it was rotten, it was rotten last night," as she strode down the hall.

One day, Hayley, Olivia, and Skeeter were the last to leave the BUGs meeting. Hayley looked out the window at the kids playing soccer. The weather was warming up. Soon it would be spring break. The trees near the school were lacy with blossoms. She saw Curtis leaning against the wall in time-out, looking sulky. The duty teacher seemed to be scolding him. *I wonder what he's done now?* Hayley thought.

As the three kids left the music room, they passed Ms. Lyons and Mr. Penwick in the hall.

Ms. Lyons was talking. "And here's our music room," she said.

"You won't need that next year," Mr. Penwick said gruffly. He patted his briefcase. "Convert it to an office. Or storage."

The grown-ups moved down the hall before Hayley could hear Ms. Lyons's reply. "What do you think

he meant?" Hayley whispered to Skeeter and Olivia. "About not needing the music room? What's going on?"

"Maybe they are going to build a bigger music room?" wondered Skeeter. "A special room for the ukulele band!"

"Not likely, Skeeter," said Hayley.

Olivia shook her head. "I'll ask my mom. Maybe she'll know."

What could Mr. Penwick mean by they wouldn't need the music room next year?

Wipeout

Over the next months, the group learned to play many songs: "Baby Bumblebee" and "Brown-Eyed Girl." They had a great time together too. Laughing. Talking. Giggling. But most of all, singing together and playing.

Playing in a group is much more fun than playing on your own, thought Hayley. The good singers carried the tune. The members with a good sense of rhythm kept the group on the beat. Someone could always cover the hard parts. And all the BUGs were great about helping each other.

And there was nothing like the big, fat sound of millions of ukuleles strumming together. Make that hundreds of ukuleles. Or thirty ukes, anyway.

One day Mr. Y held up his hand for silence. Everyone stopped playing and looked up.

"We're ready to play our first concert," he said.

"We'll perform at the Bridgewater Senior Center. Meet in the music room at 11:00 on Saturday. We'll play at noon. They'll give us lunch, and we'll ride the bus back to school."

"Our first gig!" said Hayley.

"The first of many, I hope," said Mr. Y. "I'm proud of all of you. The BUGs are growing into a fine band."

"I'm going to paint my fingernails red to match my BUGs T-shirt," said Olivia. "Lupe, you should do that too."

"Okay," said Lupe. "Come over to my house on Friday. You too, Hayley."

Hayley had noticed Lupe was using a lot more English now and making more friends. Mrs. McCann was right. The band was good for her.

In fact, the band was good for all of them. Rich kids and poor kids. Big kids and little kids. Kids who got straight As and kids who were usually found in the principal's office. Kids who'd never hung out together before. They all seemed to find a home in the uke band.

She just wished Curtis would join. Curtis needed the BUGs. She knew it.

Thursday afternoon Hayley was out in front of her house, watering the tulips. They'd had a dry spring, and everything looked dusty and wilted.

Skeeter whizzed past on his skateboard, strumming his green uke. "Look at me! I'm a surfer!" he yelled. He launched a solo from their new song. The song Olivia, Skeeter, and Hayley planned to play together at the senior center. Their spotlight trio number.

Hayley turned back to the tulips. No need to watch. Skeeter was always acting weird. *Bam!* She heard the skateboard crash.

Skeeter was on the ground. The skateboard was on the ground. His uke was on the ground in two pieces.

"I think it's broken," he said.

"Yup," said Hayley, looking at the uke. "It's broken, all right."

"No, I mean my arm." He held his wrist, which was bent at a funny angle. His eyes filled with tears. Hayley didn't believe it. Skeeter was always exaggerating. He always thought something was broken. But just in case… "I'll get Mom," she said.

The next day Skeeter came to school with his wrist in a cast.

"Oh, Skeeter," said Hayley when she saw him in the hall.

"What happened?" asked Olivia.

"Skateboard," said Skeeter. "You should have seen me! I was practically upside down and then—*Bam!* I was just down."

"But Skeeter!" said Olivia. "What about our trio? You have the solo. And our gig is tomorrow!"

"Too bad we aren't playing 'Wipeout,'" joked Skeeter. "Because I really wiped out!" He shook his hand and winced.

"We'll have to cut our trio number," Olivia said. "We can't play it without your part."

"No!" said Hayley. She didn't want to cut it. It was her favorite song. But there didn't seem to be anything else to do.

Salvation came in the form of Ms. Lyons. The BUGs meeting was just starting. The principal propelled Curtis into the music room. Ms. Lyons didn't look happy. Neither did Curtis. But he did have his ukulele case.

"You have a new member!" Ms. Lyons announced.

Mr. Y looked surprised. "You want to join BUGs?" he asked Curtis.

Curtis glared at the floor. Ms. Lyons nudged him. Curtis sighed. "Yes." He paused. "I guess."

"Remember our bargain," said Ms. Lyons. She squeezed Curtis's shoulder and left.

"This is great!" said Hayley. "You can play Skeeter's solo! What made you change your mind about joining?"

"Change my mind?" Curtis made a face. "I didn't change my mind. It was this or Ceramics Club. Ms. Lyons said."

Still, it was a good thing for BUGs. Curtis picked up Skeeter's solo in record time. And as rehearsal went on, the sullen look left his face. Soon he was tapping his toe in time to the music. And smiling! Well, maybe not smiling exactly, but he didn't look like an old grump anymore.

Hayley went over to him after rehearsal. Curtis

was stowing his uke in his case. "You never told me how you learned to play," she said.

This time Curtis really did smile. "In Hawaii," he said. "My dad was stationed there in the Navy."

"Hawaii!" Skeeter's mouth dropped open. "Wow. Palm trees! Hula girls! I'll bet you miss it."

Curtis's face shut down again. He zipped up his uke case and shouldered it. "Yeah," he said. And left.

Bad News

The BUGs rode back to school from the Bridgewater Senior Center on the school bus.

On the way over, everyone had been quiet. A little bit nervous. A little bit scared. Their first real gig! Would they remember their songs? Would the audience like them?

Hayley sat with Skeeter and Olivia. Curtis flopped down in the front seat. He stared out the window. Mr. Y sat next to him. Hayley overheard Curtis say, "I miss my old friends in Hawaii." But then Olivia said something to her, and she didn't hear any more.

But now, after the gig, the bus was filled with happy, excited voices.

"That was so cool!" said Lupe. "Best time ever!"

"Did you see that couple dancing? Our music made them get up and dance!" shouted Devon.

"An old man told me that he used to play the ukulele," said Hayley. "Mr. Benson. He was nice."

"They really liked it, you could tell!" Skeeter laughed. Skeeter had gone along, in spite of his broken wrist. Mr. Y had given him a maraca to shake and told him he was a percussionist.

"One lady pinched my cheek," giggled Olivia. "She said I was adorable!"

"And you are!" cooed Skeeter, batting his eyes. Olivia poked him in the ribs with her elbow. He laughed.

"Did you hear everybody clapping?" said Hayley, ignoring their horseplay. "They didn't want us to stop."

Even Curtis managed a smile when Mr. Y gave him a high five. "Great solo, man! You brought down the house."

"You're one of us now," said Hayley. "A BUG!"

Curtis grinned and ducked his head. The grumpy frown lines between his eyes were gone.

Hayley looked around at all the happy kids. She gloated. *Look at Lupe, chattering away to Michelle. Look at Curtis, smiling.*

She was the one who had started the BUGs. Maybe nobody else remembered it had been Hayley's idea. It didn't matter. No one ever called her shrimp now!

The bus dropped the kids off in the school parking lot. Parents waited. The kids ran off, still talking.

Hayley spotted Dad's truck. She waved goodbye to her friends and climbed in. Olivia started to get in her mom's car. Suddenly she ran back.

"Hayley!" she yelled.

Hayley rolled down the window. "What's up?"

Olivia paused to catch her breath. "Bad news," she finally gasped. "About the music program. About Mr. Y!" Olivia's mom called and she turned. "Just a minute, Mom!" she yelled.

Olivia grabbed Hayley's hand. "There's an emergency school board meeting tonight at seven at the school district office. You've got to come." She looked at Hayley's dad. "You, too, Mr. Godwin!" Her eyes were wide. "They're going to cut our music program!"

All five of the school board members were seated when Hayley and her family walked in to the boardroom. Three women and two men sat behind a long table, facing the room. Hayley recognized Mr. Penwick, the school board president. He wore his usual sour expression. She didn't know the others.

Mom, Dad, Hayley, and Tilly sat in the front row. Tilly perched on the edge of her chair. Her feet dangled above the floor. She clutched Bun-Bun. She had promised to be quiet. But Hayley hoped the meeting would be short. She wasn't sure how long Tilly could hold out.

Olivia was there, with her mom. Olivia gave a tiny wave when she saw Hayley. Hayley waved back. The boardroom was nearly empty except for a scattering of adults. No one else that Hayley knew.

Mr. Penwick started the meeting by opening his briefcase and taking out some papers. He put on his horn-rimmed glasses and peered over the tops.

Hayley listened for a while. Phrases like *"proposed budget cuts," "eliminate one FTE,"* and *"standardized testing"* floated through her mind. The room was stuffy. Hayley dozed off. She woke when she heard the words, *music program.*

"Cut the elementary music program," Mr. Penwick was saying. "Save money."

"But music is important!" argued one school board member.

"No one cares about the program," said Mr. Penwick. He gestured to the nearly empty room. "See, no one even came to support it. The kids can listen to CDs, or ear pods, or whatever they call that stuff. That's all they do these days, anyway."

There was more discussion. Olivia's mom stood up and talked about how music improves test scores. Mr. Penwick yawned.

Dad stood up and talked about music and art and becoming a well-rounded adult. Mr. Penwick doo- dled on the pad of paper in front of him.

Mom stood up and talked about Mr. Yaeger. How he knew all the kids in school. How he helped them. Hayley was proud of both of her parents, but Mr. Pen- wick just looked bored.

A few other people spoke, some in favor of cutting music, some against. "We've got no choice!" insisted one citizen. "We have to balance the budget!" At last the board voted. Three to two. And—just like that— Bridgewater Elementary School lost its music pro- gram. Mr. Penwick declared the meeting over and snapped his briefcase shut.

Hayley and her family left the meeting too unhappy to talk.

Hayley was quiet on the car ride home. No more music program. No more BUGs. No concerts. No gigs. No more Mr. Y with his silly jokes and his colorful vests.

The thought hit her, and she shot straight up in her seat.

No more Mr. Y! What would become of him?

12

A Brilliant Plan?

The news spread quickly through the school. The BUGs filed silently into the music room. What a change from Saturday! After the concert at the senior center, everyone had bubbled over with high spirits. Now Hayley felt as flat and gray as the April rain that streaked the windows.

Even Mr. Y looked different. His vest was a drab green. The sparkle was gone from his eyes. His bow tie wilted.

"Why do they have to cut *music*?" wailed Hayley as she tuned her uke. "Why not cut *math* instead? Nobody likes math!"

"Hey!" said Skeeter. "I do."

Olivia rolled her eyes. "You would, Skeeter."

Skeeter ignored Olivia's dig. "What will happen to *you*, Mr. Yaeger?" he asked. Hayley noticed that Skeeter used his full name, something he never, ever did.

"Well," said Mr. Y, "I guess I'll need to look for a

new job." He picked up a book from his desk. And set it back down. He shook his head as if to shake away painful thoughts. "Hey. No BUGs meeting today, okay? I need some time to process this."

The BUGs left sadly. No one talked. No one played. They just. Walked. Out.

"Mr. Y just bought a house," whispered Olivia to Hayley when they were out in the hallway. "They have a new baby."

Hayley's eyes widened. Her dad's job had been cut last year. She knew what that did to a family. "Will they have to sell their house? Move?"

Olivia shook her head. "I don't know."

That night, Hayley lay in bed, too worried to sleep. Her nightlight made a yellow glow on the wall. Mango and Tango were curled up like orange puffballs in their tank. They were sound asleep. But Hayley's stomach was tied in knots.

She felt awful about the music program. But what could she do? She was just one eight-year-old girl. One little, ukulele-playing third grader.

Light reflected from the picture frame on her dresser. A copy of Ruby's photo from the family album. Mom had it framed for her after the talent show.

Ruby and Her Ragtime Rascals. Ruby didn't let polio stop her.

Ruby wouldn't give up. Neither would Hayley. The fight wasn't over yet. Not by a long shot. Who said she was too little? She was Ukulele Hayley! The leader of the BUGs!

She fell asleep and woke up in the morning with a brilliant idea. Well, nearly brilliant. Make that possibly brilliant.

She hummed all the way to school. With Ms. Lyons's permission, she made an announcement over the loudspeaker. "Attention, BUGs!" she said. "Emergency meeting! Noon! By the soccer field!" Her voice didn't crack. Not once!

At lunch recess Hayley walked across the playground with Skeeter and Olivia. Meeting time! Time for the brilliant idea! They passed Josh and Curtis sitting on the ground. They were doing something with little round pieces of cardboard. Skeeter stopped. "Whatcha doing?" he asked.

Josh looked up. "Curtis is teaching me to play pogs," he said.

"It's a game from Hawaii," said Curtis.

"Well, play it later," said Olivia. "It's time for our meeting!"

The BUGs gathered by the soccer field. Hayley took charge. "The school board is cutting our music program," she told them. "But the vote was close. Maybe we can change their minds. The next school board meeting is May 7. We need to do something."

"Let's TP Mr. Penwick's house!" said Skeeter. Olivia rolled her eyes.

"Don't be silly, Skeeter," said Hayley. "We don't want to make things worse.

"I was thinking," Hayley continued. She paused. She wanted to make this sound good to convince the BUGs. "Let's give a concert right before the meeting, in front of the district office building. The school board will walk by and hear us. They'll see how good we are. They'll see we care." She waited anxiously to hear what the BUGs would say.

There was a minute while everyone thought about it.

"If all the kids from school and their parents came, the board would see how important music is," said Devon slowly.

"And what Mr. Y helped us do," Lupe said.

"Yes!" said Olivia. Her eyes shone. "Let's get our parents to come, maybe grandparents, aunts, and uncles. Brothers and sisters. Neighbors. Everyone! The more people, the better. A big crowd!"

"And we can have some signs," said Lupe.

"Balloons!" yelled Josh.

"Posters, all over town!" shouted Anna.

Skeeter jumped up and down. "I can see it now! Humongous crowd! Hundreds, no—thousands! Maybe a million people!"

"Are there that many people in our neighborhood?" asked Michelle.

"No!" Robert laughed. "But a couple of hundred would look pretty good."

Curtis looked thoughtful. "My mom is a reporter.

Maybe she'd come and take pictures. Then we'd be in the paper."

The bell rang, and the BUGs headed back to their classes, buzzing like bees with ideas for the rally.

Hayley stared into the distance, eyes shining. A new idea—even more brilliant than the last—was taking shape.

Easier said than done. Just like learning the uke. Just like playing in the talent show. Just like starting a band.

So many things are like that, thought Hayley. She painted SAVE OUR MUSIC PROGRAM in slightly straggly letters on a big piece of poster board.

"We need more black paint!" shouted Olivia from the corner of the garage. She and Lupe and Skeeter were painting signs too. Skeeter's read DON'T STOP THE MUSIC, just like their new yellow T-shirts.

Hayley sighed. She was tired already, and the rally was still a few days away.

Easier said than done. But another saying came to mind as well. Something Dad used to say when he needed help cleaning up the kitchen after dinner: *Many hands make light work.*

And so it was with the rally. All the BUGs helped. It turned out that you couldn't just hold a rally any old time you wanted to. You had to get permission. So Dad took Hayley and Olivia down to City Hall and helped them fill out the application.

Then the BUGs had to make flyers and posters to advertise the rally and hand them out at the shopping

center. They took them to every store and posted them in the windows. They addressed and stamped hundreds of flyers. They made banners and inflated balloons and ordered T-shirts.

And rehearsed, of course. It wouldn't impress the school board one bit if the band wasn't any good!

Once the word got out, lots of kids from school wanted to help. Parents and teachers too. Dad made an e-mail list of parent helpers, and Mom started a phone tree. Parents and kids wrote letters to the editor and to the school board. Curtis told his mom about the rally, and she arranged for her newspaper to cover the event.

Many hands make light work. It was true. The work went quickly with so many people—kids, BUGs, parents, and friends—helping.

But would it be enough to make a difference?

13

Don't Stop the Music

Hayley woke to a soft pattering sound. Mango and Tango nibbling their kibbles? Tilly tiptoeing in the hall? Then she realized what it was—rain! And on the day of the rally!

She pictured the BUGs with water dripping off their ukuleles and wind blowing music off their stands. Thunder drowning out their singing. No one would come to the rally in the rain.

She stomped into the kitchen feeling like an old grouch. Tilly padded down the hall behind her. "Breakfast, Sissy?" she asked.

Hayley got out the bowls and spoons. She poured them each a bowl of cereal. The milk was in a special pitcher that wasn't too heavy. She tipped it carefully, tucking her tongue between her teeth as she poured.

The hours crawled by. Hayley finished her homework. She made her bed. She took her dirty clothes out to the laundry room. She practiced her ukulele.

In between chores, she glared out the window. If only the stupid rain would stop!

By five o'clock, she got her wish. The sun broke through. Mount Hood peeked through the clouds.

"Dad!" she yelled. "The mountain is out!" She danced around in her bare feet, too excited to eat dinner. "Hurry up!" she told her parents. "We can't be late!"

At last, everyone had finished eating. Tilly and Hayley helped Dad clean up. It took forever. Finally, the kitchen was spotless, the way Dad liked it. Hayley pulled on her yellow DON'T STOP THE MUSIC T-shirt and grabbed her ukulele. Rally time!

Would anyone come?

Would they! Would they ever! When Hayley and her family arrived at the district office, there were so many cars that there was no place to park. Dad dropped Hayley, Tilly, and Mom off and went to find a parking space.

From the sidewalk, Hayley looked across to the school district office building. It was an old brick building. Stone steps led up to a wide porch, forming a space almost as big as a stage. This is where the BUGs had decided to hold the concert. The school board members would have to walk right past them to get to the meeting. They couldn't help but notice the band.

Now, as Hayley wound her way through the crowd, she wondered if anyone else would be able to see! The lawn in front of the district office was packed with people. Some carried signs. Some held balloons. Some wore yellow T-shirts like hers.

Hayley spotted Skeeter and Olivia. She grabbed her uke. "See you later!" she called to Mom and Tilly. She ran off to meet the rest of the BUGs.

"Look!" said Olivia. "Anna Chee from *Channel Seven News* is here!" She pointed to a van. Anna Chee was Olivia's favorite reporter because she was Chinese American too. "We're going to be on TV!"

A dark-haired woman was setting up a camera and a microphone. Hayley grinned, but she wasn't surprised.

"That was my brilliant idea!" she exclaimed. "The one I was keeping a secret! I called the TV station!" Hayley hadn't told anyone—not even her parents— because she didn't want to disappoint them if it didn't work out. But here was Anna Chee in person!

"Come on!" Hayley pulled Skeeter and Olivia over. Then she stood there, shyly, until the reporter introduced herself.

"So you're the little girl with the big ideas? I'm Anna Chee." Ms. Chee had a dazzling smile and glossy hair. She was even prettier in person than on TV. "I'd like to interview you."

On camera, Hayley told all about learning to play the ukulele and starting the BUGs with Mr. Y's help. She told how important the music program was. She was too caught up in her story to have time to feel even one bit shy.

"Well, Ukulele Hayley, I understand that you're the little girl responsible for this rally," said Ms. Chee. "What made a third grader think she could do this?"

Hayley told Anna Chee the story of Ruby and Her Ragtime Rascals. "She did all that in a leg brace," Hayley continued. "Because she was determined. I knew if she could do that, I could do this. But I didn't do it all alone. Lots of people helped."

"Were you worried that no one would come?"

Hayley smiled. "Never," she said. "Well, maybe. Make that some of the time." She took a deep breath. "Well, actually I worried all the time. But I guess lots of people believe in the power of music too."

It was time to start. Hayley joined the rest of the BUGs on the steps. She looked out over the crowd. It was amazing to see all the parents and kids, teachers, friends, and neighbors. Mrs. McCann was there. So was Ms. Lyons. She spotted Mom and Dad, with Tilly on his shoulders. Hayley grinned and waved. Mom cheered. Dad gave her a thumbs-up.

Olivia's mom stepped up to the microphone to introduce the BUGs. "If the music program is cut," she said, "this is just one of the talented student groups that we will lose."

The thirty-five members, dressed in yellow T-shirts, stood at attention. At Mr. Y's signal, they began. They played and sang, strummed and hummed. Curtis played a solo. Hayley, Skeeter, and Olivia played their trio piece.

There were a few glitches—what live performance doesn't have a few glitches? But Hayley thought it was the best they'd ever sounded. They ended with a song that Michelle had written for the rally:

Don't stop the music, they sang. *Let it ring!*
Don't stop the music! Let us sing.

They took their bows to applause and cheers.

Then, the members of the school board came onstage. Mr. Penwick took the microphone. He looked as cross as ever. He tapped the mic to make sure it was on. Then he cleared his throat. "First of all, I'd like to say that I'm impressed by this outpouring of support for the music program." He paused, and Hayley's heart pounded. *It isn't going to work,* she thought. *The board is going to cut the program anyway. What will I do without the BUGs?* She reached out and grabbed Olivia's hand and squeezed it.

Mr. Penwick continued. "Obviously, we've underestimated the importance of music to the Bridgewater Elementary community. The board will reconsider the program and take another vote." With that, the school board filed inside.

14

Ukulele Hayley and Her BUGs

Hayley started to follow the school board members, but Mom pulled her back. Tilly was slumped over Mom's shoulder, snoring gently. "It's late," Mom said. "We need to get Tilly home to bed."

Hayley's face fell. She *had* to know how the school board would vote!

Dad agreed. "Let's give Hayley a chance to see this through," he said. "She's worked so hard. Take Tilly home and I'll wait with Hayley. We'll catch a ride with the Watsons after the meeting."

Mom nodded. "I want you to know that whatever they decide, we are very proud of you," she said. She dropped a kiss on the top of Hayley's head and carried Tilly across the lawn to the car. Dad and Hayley went into the district office.

The room was packed. Skeeter and his grandmother were there, as well as Olivia and Mr. and Mrs. Watson and most of the other BUGs. Even Curtis.

Every chair was filled. Ms. Lyons sat in front, with Mr. Y and Mrs. McCann. Standing room only. Hayley and Dad leaned against the back wall.

Mr. Penwick called the meeting to order.

"First of all," he said, "I'd like to recognize the parents, teachers, and students here tonight and thank them for coming. We have changed our agenda to take another vote on cutting the music program."

"Just a minute, Mr. Chairman!" another board member spoke up. "Before we vote, take a look at this!" She handed Mr. Penwick a piece of paper. He put on his glasses and peered at it for a moment. Then he whipped a calculator out and punched in numbers. His usual sour expression dissolved into a big smile.

"We've just been informed that The Benson Charitable Trust will award a grant to the Bridgewater Ukulele Group!" he announced. "However, the grant will be given only if the school music program is kept open."

Benson Trust? Could that be the same sweet old Mr. Benson from the senior center? The one who used to play the uke? Hayley looked around the room. She spotted him—a thin old man with a big grin. He caught her eye and winked.

The board took a vote. This time, all five members voted to keep the music program. The room erupted with cheers. "Hooray!" shouted Skeeter.

Mr. Penwick banged his gavel for silence. "The board has voted to reinstate the music program. After a short recess, we will continue our meeting to look for ways to save money elsewhere."

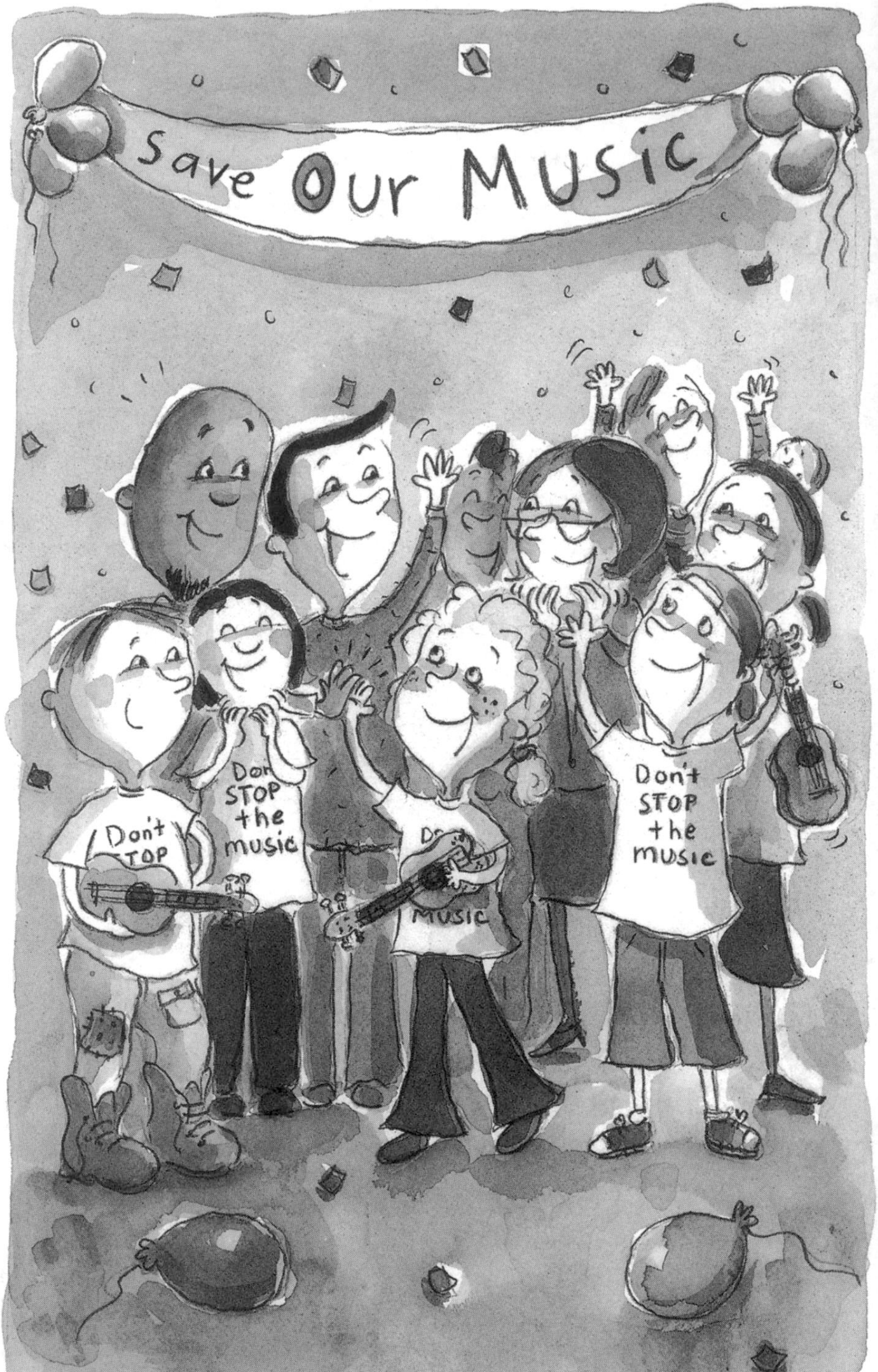
Save Our Music
Don't STOP the music

The school board recessed for fifteen minutes. As the crowd streamed out, people stopped to congratulate Hayley. Mrs. McCann gave her a hug. Ms. Lyons had tears in her eyes as she shook Hayley's hand. Mr. Y gave her a high five. Hayley glowed. She floated out of the boardroom and followed Dad down the stairs.

When she got back home, Jennifer and Sam were on the phone, calling for Hayley. From college!

"I saw the rally on TV!" Jennifer said. "Hayley, you are a shining star."

"We're proud of you," said Sam. "Way to go!"

Hayley beamed as she hung up the phone. Not too little! Not the shrimp! Not Go-Away-Hayley anymore!

On Monday Mr. Y met the BUGs at the door of the music room with a big grin.

The kids all crowded around. By now everyone had heard the news. But they wanted to hear it again.

"Yes," Mr. Y said. "The music program will stay! And so will I!"

"This calls for a celebration!" shouted Skeeter.

"What should we do to celebrate?" asked Lupe.

"What else?" said Hayley, picking up her uke. "Let's rock!"

Hayley's Tips on
How to Play the Ukulele

The ukulele is an easy instrument to learn to play. It's light, portable, and small. Best of all, it's inexpensive. Unlike the guitar, it has only four strings. Unlike the recorder, you can sing with it while you play.

Choosing a Uke

Although Hayley found a nice ukulele at a garage sale, you might do better at a music store. Don't buy a plastic toy uke. You won't be happy with the tone, and they are hard to play. Use nylon strings on your ukulele. Steel strings will be too tight and might bend the neck.

How to Hold Your Ukulele

Hold the uke lightly against your rib cage with the neck in your left hand. Put your left thumb gently on the back of the neck, and curl your fingers around it to touch the strings. Your right arm holds the uke. Use your right fingers for strumming and your left hand to press the strings down to play chords.

Tuning the Uke

You will also want to get a tuner. A digital tuner that clamps to the top of the ukulele is a good investment. Playing out of tune is not fun! Remember, you can tune a uke, but you can't tuna fish!

Turn the tuning peg with your left hand until the string matches the pitch you want. There are different tunings you can use, but most soprano ukes use C tuning. The strings are tuned to GCEA. You can remember the notes with "Good Cooks Eat A lot." If you don't have a tuner, you can tune to a piano. When your uke is in tune, it will sound like the tune of "My Dog Has Fleas." Sing along to hear the notes the strings should make.

Strumming

To get started, use your pointer finger to softly strum across all the strings. You can vary the rhythm by strumming upward as well. There are many different strumming patterns you can use. Internet videos are a good place to watch people demonstrate different strums.

First Chord—C

You really can play hundreds of songs with just three chords. Start with C. Put the third finger of your left hand on the A string at the third fret. That's a C chord! See how easy it is? You can find diagrams for other chords on the Internet or from a ukulele book.